LOVE ON WARD B

**HOSPITAL
NURSE
PICTURE
LIBRARY**

The publishers would like to thank the team at IPC Media Ltd and DC Comics for their help in compiling this book, particularly David Abbott and Linda Lee.

Published in 2008 by Prion
An imprint of the Carlton Publishing Group
20 Mortimer Street
London W1T 3JW

A catalogue record for this book is available from the British Library.

ISBN 978-1-85375-666-5

Printed and bound in Dubai
10 9 8 7 6 5 4 3 2 1

LOVE ON WARD B

**HOSPITAL
NURSE
PICTURE
LIBRARY**

6 OF THE
BEST HOSPITAL NURSE
PICTURE LIBRARY ROMANCES
EVER!

PRION

CONTENTS

NAUGHTY NURSE
6

FIRST LOVE
71

MAN CRAZY
137

CURE FOR DIANE
203

LIVE AND LOVE
269

BLUES FOR A BEAT BOY
335

INTRODUCTION

Blonde and impossibly beautiful, Sally Brown is a probationary nurse at General Hospital and the star of *Hospital Nurse Picture Library*. With her friend and colleague Maureen Evans she patrols the kind of wards that would have been familiar to her readers thanks to television. *Emergency Ward 10* had been running since 1957 so everyone knew that hospitals were buildings full of dishy doctors and patients in need of a little tender loving care.

Where better to find romance and drama than in a hospital? 'A life in our hands! What a responsibility, and what a challenge!' thinks Sally. Sally is 'the serious one' according to one of her writers, although in truth she's sensible rather than serious. She likes an evening out at a club or a romantic dinner as much as the next girl — unless the next girl is Maureen, of course, because Maureen has a habit of finding trouble as often as she changes her hair colour (blonde one story, brunette the next). Maureen, in her fun-loving way, is more of a dreamer, persuaded to become a nurse after seeing a television programme, but a good nurse nonetheless.

Working on the wards isn't easy and Matron's word is law: 'Observe and learn,' she is wont to say. 'Alertness and efficiency will help you become the sort of assistants a surgeon expects to have in the operating theatre.' Yet even the starched apron of a Hospital Matron can hide deep feelings, as you will see in the stories that follow.

As probationary nurses, Sally and Maureen find themselves moved around General Hospital to wherever the plot needed them to be, whether it was the children's ward or a surgical ward. This was the 'local' hospital, so it's something of a miracle that so many stars and celebrities turn up in its whitewashed corridors. Actresses, dancers, pop stars — even footballers, long before the tabloid-created term WAG came into fashion. Sally was even concerned over slimming pills years before today's size zero culture.

Dizzy newcomers to the wards are sent into a spin at the first sight of a handsome patient or doctor. And such doctors: at General Hospital you could guarantee that they were handsome and fashionably smart. They liked romantic dates, dancing and . . . but wait . . . it wasn't all tender first kisses and 'happy ever after' for nurse Sally. All too often, the intelligent, devoted, handsome doctor had a dark secret that would thwart romance at every turn. Emotionally, they were distant and required the same tending and nurturing that Sally offered her patients.

Everyone in these stories was beautiful, as if the artists were incapable of drawing anything less than perfection. Sally's world did not involve bedpans or MRSA.

For decades, nursing was second only to being an air hostess when it came to glamorous occupations for girls. Tales like 'First Love' and 'Live and Love' tap into the obvious elements of love and romance—but titles like 'Man Crazy' and 'Naughty Nurse' hint that there is more fun to be had in these picture stories than between the prim covers of a Mills & Boon novel.

If you think hospitals are just sterile wards full of sick people, think again.

Melissa Hyland

HOSPITAL NURSE PICTURE LIBRARY

PEARSON'S

AN OFFBEAT ROMANCE
FOR NURSE SALLY BROWN

1/-

NAUGHTY NURSE

MAUREEN GIGGLED AND DID NOT AT ONCE NOTICE THE ARRIVAL OF ONE OF THE HOSPITAL'S MALE NURSES.

EXCUSE ME, BUT I MUST INTERRUPT.

MR. GALE'S X-RAYS ARE NEEDED. DR. MOORE IS ASKING FOR THEM. HE NEEDS THEM FOR THE OP.

NOT TO WORRY. I HAVE THEM HERE.

WHO'S THAT?

REGGIE, A MALE NURSE. HE'S VERY STUDIOUS — HOPES TO BE A CHIROPODIST WITH HIS OWN SURGERY, ONE DAY.

HOW ABOUT IT, JOYCE? WAS IT BETTER THAT TIME?

YES, SAL. I THINK I'M GOING TO BE ALL RIGHT NOW, THANKS TO YOU.

I'VE BEEN A COWARD ALL MY LIFE, BUT FOR ONCE I'VE FACED UP TO REALITY, AND I FEEL A WHOLE LOT HAPPIER.

THAT WAS ONLY THE FIRST OBSTACLE, SALLY REALISED THAT OTHERS STILL REMAINED... REGGIE, FOR INSTANCE.

FIRST TIME I'VE SEEN OUR REGGIE STARING AT A COUPLE OF GIRLS. WE SHOULD FEEL FLATTERED, JOYCE.

AND AS SALLY HAD EXPECTED.

ALL RIGHT YOU MIGHT HAVE THE KNOW-HOW SO FAR AS NURSING IS CONCERNED. BUT WHEN IT COMES TO MY PRIVATE LIFE, I'LL ASK YOU NOT TO INTERFERE.

JOYCE HAD COME TO HER OWN CONCLUSION.

THEY'RE JEALOUS. THEY WANT THOMAS TO TAKE NOTICE OF THEM, TOO.

JUST THEN THEY HEARD THE CLICK-CLICK OF STEEL TIPPED HEELS. SALLY KNEW IT WAS JOYCE... SISTER HAD ALREADY MADE A SCATHING COMMENT ABOUT HER SHOES...

REGGIE SHOULD HAVE FINISHED THAT DRESSING BY NOW AND THOMAS WILL BE ON HIS OWN.

SALLY PAUSED... WAITING FOR THE RIGHT MOMENT.

I'LL SHOW HER THAT THOMAS IS A NO-GOOD CASANOVA.

REGGIE'S PEP TALK DID JOYCE A LOT OF GOOD. SHE BECAME MORE UNDERSTANDING, AND HER FEELINGS TOWARDS HIM GREW DAILY...

YOU SHOULD BE OFF DUTY NOW, REGGIE. WOULD YOU LIKE ME TO FINISH THAT DRESSING FOR YOU?

THANKS ALL THE SAME, JOYCE, BUT I HAPPEN TO KNOW THAT THIS IS YOUR HALF-DAY. GO AND GET SOME REST.

BUT I DON'T FEEL TIRED...HONESTLY I DON'T.

EVEN IF I TOLD HER THE REAL REASON FOR MY BEHAVIOUR I COULDN'T MAKE HER UNDERSTAND THAT IT WAS FOR HER OWN GOOD. THE TROUBLE IS THAT THOMAS REALLY DOES SEEM TO HAVE FALLEN IN LOVE WITH ME. THINGS ARE GETTING OUT OF HAND.

POOR SALLY WAS IN TROUBLE. SHE HAD PLAYED UP TO THOMAS TO TEACH JOYCE A LESSON AND NOW NOT ONLY WAS JOYCE HOSTILE BUT MAUREEN TOO. IT WAS ALL A GIRL COULD STAND.

WELL DID YOU MANAGE TO KISS YOUR BOYFRIEND BEFORE HE WAS TUCKED UP FOR THE NIGHT?

YOU OUGHT TO KNOW ME BETTER THAN THAT MAUREEN.

WHY SHOULD I? I'M THE FEATHER-BRAINED ONE, REMEMBER? WHEN I FALL FOR THOMAS MITCHELL, I'M CRAZY, BUT YOU...

DON'T BE LIKE THAT MAUREEN. I NEED A FRIEND CAN'T YOU SEE THAT I'M TRYING TO HELP JOYCE AND REGGIE TO COME TOGETHER.

WELL, I MUST SAY IT'S THE STRANGEST WAY OF HELPING TWO PEOPLE THAT I'VE HEARD OF.

WOULDN'T BE THAT THIS IS PART OF YOUR LITTLE SCHEME TO GET THOMAS TO YOURSELF WOULD IT?

OH, DEAR, I'M NOT SURE OF ANYTHING ANY MORE.

AT FIRST I THOUGHT IT WAS EASY TO HAVE A LITTLE FLIRTATION WITH HIM, BELIEVING THOMAS TO BE SELFISH AND CONCEITED, BUT NOW I REALISE THAT HE HAS SUFFERED A BIG HURT WHICH MAKES HIM ACT THIS WAY.

ARE YOU TRYING TO SAY THAT THOMAS IS SUFFERING FROM A HEARTACHE WHICH MAKES HIM WHISPER SWEET NOTHINGS INTO THE EARS OF EVERY GIRL HE MEETS?

YES, I AM.

SO SALLY LEFT, LEAVING URSULA TO A GREAT DEAL OF HEART SEARCHING...

NO, NO. WHY SHOULD I EAT HUMBLE PIE TO GO AND SEE HIM?

SALLY DID NOT MENTION TO THOMAS HER MEETING WITH URSULA, EVEN THOUGH HE BECAME DAILY MORE ATTENTIVE.

I'VE GOT A NEW LOOK ON LIFE SINCE I'VE MET YOU, SAL.

THINGS COULD HAVE BEEN SO DIFFERENT FOR SALLY, BUT SHE KNEW THAT URSULA'S MEMORY WOULD HAVE ALWAYS REMAINED WITH THOMAS, CREATING A BARRIER BETWEEN HIMSELF AND THE GIRL WHO BECAME HIS WIFE. NOW HE WOULD BE MARRYING FOR LOVE, OF THAT SALLY WAS CONVINCED.

IT'S BETTER THIS WAY, AND I DID HELP A LITTLE. I WISH I COULD DO THE SAME FOR REGGIE AND JOYCE.

SALLY TURNED TO GO BACK INTO THE HOSPITAL AND BUMPED INTO THE GIRL SHE HAD BEEN THINKING ABOUT.

I'VE BEEN SPYING ON YOU SALLY, AND TELLING YOU THAT, I WANT TO APOLOGISE.

I SAW YOU REFUSE THOMAS. OH, SAL, YOU'RE THE GREATEST.

I ONLY FLIRTED WITH THOMAS BECAUSE I WANTED YOU TO REALISE HOW NICE A FELLOW REGGIE IS.

PEARSON'S

HOSPITAL NURSE PICTURE LIBRARY

NURSE SALLY BROWN IN

1/-

FIRST LOVE

LIVING AND
LOVING
IS MORE
THAN
A GAME

BUT MAUREEN SEEMED DETERMINED TO MAKE HER PRESENCE FELT....

GOOD OL' BERT HOORAY

BERT BECAME SUDDENLY CONSCIOUS OF MAUREEN'S VOICE ABOVE THE REST... AND IN A LULL IN THE GAME...

YOO-HOO, MAUREEN. I'M GLAD YOU MADE IT

THE GIRL WHOM THEY BOTH LOVED, WATCHED FROM THE STANDS

YOUR TWO ADMIRERS APPEAR TO BE LOSING CONTROL

THEY BOTH HAD A REPUTATION FOR CLEVER FOOTWORK, BUT ON THIS OCCASION . . .

AAAGH!

THE UNLUCKY ONE WAS CARRIED OFF THE FIELD, WHILE THE SPECTATORS AND PLAYERS WATCHED SILENTLY

THEN BERT WAS OFF ON HIS FAVOURITE TOPIC OF CONVERSATION....

DID YOU SEE THE WAY THEY SLAMMED THE BALL ACROSS TO ME HONEY?

I CERTAINLY DID. I RECKON I WAS A GOOD MASCOT FOR YOU THIS AFTERNOON

I'LL LEAVE YOU TWO TO WHISPER SWEET NOTHINGS TO EACH OTHER

YOU DON'T HAVE TO GO, SAL

BUT SALLY WAS ANXIOUS TO FIND OUT THE LATEST ON PERCY PEARMAN, RECENTLY ADMITTED TO THE GENERAL HOSPITAL

I'LL HELP IF I CAN. WHO IS IT?

ELSIE, WOULD YOU MIND ME LOOKING AT ONE OF THE PATIENT'S ADMISSION CARDS, PLEASE?

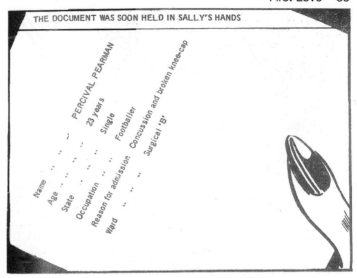

HE'S TOO EXCITED, HE NEEDS A SEDATIVE

HE MUST BE VERY MUCH IN LOVE WITH THIS CLARISSA GIRL

AFTER THAT IT WAS BED FOR SALLY, BUT SHE WAS STILL AWAKE WHEN MAUREEN RETURNED HOME

OH, WE'VE HAD SUCH A MARVELLOUS TIME

YES HE DID....

LET ME GUESS., YOU'VE HAD A NON-STOP TWISTING SESSION. BUT TELL ME, DID BERT MENTION PERCY AGAIN?

SO FAR, HE'S ONLY MUTTERED THAT IT'S A DIFFICULT CASE. BUT YOU'VE GOT SOMETHING THERE, MAUREEN. I'LL SEE IF HE'S FREE NOW

TRUST SAL. ALWAYS A CHAMPION IN SOMEONE ELSE'S CAUSE

THE DOCTOR WAS NOT VERY OPTIMISTIC......

YOU SHOULD KNOW WHAT HAPPENS, NURSE BROWN. AFTER SURGERY THE KNEE-CAP BECOMES STIFF, AND IT IS NOT UNTIL MUCH LATER THAT WE CAN BE CERTAIN OF ITS USEFUL-NESS. PEARMAN MAY NEVER BE ABLE TO PLAY FOOTBALL AGAIN

THE GIRL WHO ANSWERED THE DOOR WAS VERY BEAUTIFUL IN A COLD, UNSYMPATHETIC SORT OF WAY

WHO ARE YOU? I DON'T USUALLY SEE STRANGERS LIKE THIS

NEITHER DO I VISIT PEOPLE I DON'T KNOW UNLESS I HAVE A SPECIAL REASON FOR DOING SO

ALL RIGHT, COME TO THE POINT, BUT BE QUICK ABOUT IT

IT'S ABOUT PERCY PEARMAN. HE'S IN HOSPITAL AND TERRIBLY DEPRESSED. A VISIT FROM YOU WOULD HELP HIM NO END

I HAVEN'T GOT GREEN EYES. WHAT'S SHE GETTING AT? PERHAPS SHE'S WRITTEN ME OFF AS BEING GREEDY. BUT THEN WHY SHOULD I CARE

SALLY'S NEXT CALL WAS AT THE SPORTS' GROUND, WHERE DAVE WAS TRAINING........

THAT GIRL COULDN'T MAKE A MAN HAPPY IF SHE TRIED

AH, THERE'S DAVE. PERHAPS HE'LL BE MORE UNDERSTANDING AND HELPFUL......AFTER ALL, HE AND PERCY USED TO BE FRIENDS BEFORE CLARISSA CAME INTO THE PICTURE

CLARISSA WILL NEVER BE MY GIRL, NOR PERCY'S FOR THAT MATTER. THE ONLY THING THAT REALLY BOTHERS ME IS THAT I'VE LET ANOTHER GIRL DOWN PRETTY BADLY

TELL ME ABOUT HER, DAVE

I MET HER IN MY HOME TOWN. MARY WAS HER NAME, AND SHE WAS REALLY CUTE

WE BELIEVED WE WERE IN LOVE WITH EACH OTHER. BUT THEN I HAD SOME SUCCESS AS A FOOTBALLER, AND WE DRIFTED APART

DAYS PASSED, AND PERCY'S JAUNDICED OUTLOOK ON LIFE DID NOT IMPROVE ON HIS FIRST DAY OUT OF BED, SALLY AND MAUREEN DISCUSSED THE SITUATION IN THE HOSPITAL CANTEEN

HE'S MAKING SOME PROGRESS ANYWAY

MMM, BUT IT ISN'T ENOUGH. TELL ME, MAUREEN, DO YOU BELIEVE IN FIRST LOVE?

I'D SAY IT ALL DEPENDS, ALTHOUGH LOTS OF YOUNG PEOPLE WHO KNEW EACH OTHER AT SCHOOL SEEM TO FIND THEIR LOVE IS THE TYPE THAT LASTS

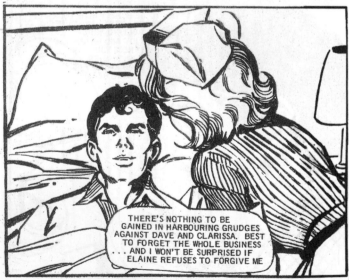

THE NEXT SIX DAYS PASSED ALL TOO QUICKLY SO FAR AS SALLY WAS CONCERNED. SHE WANTED TO HOLD THEM BACK, NOT TO LET THEM GO . . .

NOW IT WAS PERCY WHO WAS BOTHERED BY SALLY'S WORRIED EXPRESSION...

WHAT'S MAKING YOU FEEL SO UNHAPPY, SAL?

NOTHING.... NOTHING IMPORTANT

HOW CAN I TELL HIM THAT AT THIS MOMENT ELAINE IS GETTING HERSELF DRESSED FOR HER WEDDING TO JIM WINTER? THIS NEWS MIGHT BRING ON ALL THE OLD DEPRESSIONS AGAIN

LOOK AT ME SAL. YOU AND I KNOW EACH OTHER WELL ENOUGH NOW. HAVE YOU SOME BAD NEWS THAT YOU'RE AFRAID TO BREAK TO ME?

THERE SEEMED TO BE SUCH A LOT OF WEDDINGS TAKING PLACE THAT SUMMER. FIRST PERCY AND ELAINE, THEN DAVE AND MARY — NOT FORGETTING BERT AND BETTY. BUT WHILE OTHER GIRLS WORE WREATHS OF ORANGE BLOSSOM, SALLY AND MAUREEN PLACED THEIR NURSES CAPS FIRMLY ON THEIR HEADS AND CARRIED ON.

HOSPITAL NURSE PICTURE LIBRARY

PEARSON'S

NURSE SALLY HAS
TROUBLE WITH A
TRAINEE WHO GOES

1'-

MAN CRAZY

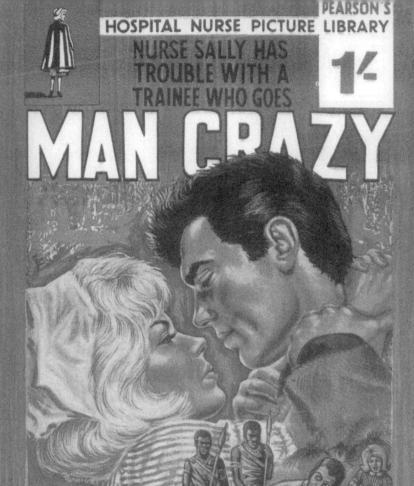

NO, APPARENTLY HE'S GOING TO THE WEST INDIES TO WORK IN A CLINIC THERE. IT WILL MEAN GIVING UP QUITE A NUMBER OF THINGS. HE MUST BE DEAD KEEN.

DEDICATED, TOO. STILL I'M SORRY HE'S GOING.

THE FOLLOWING DAY, THE NEW PROBATIONARY NURSES ARRIVED. THEY WERE A MIXED CROWD... SOME APPEARED NERVOUS   WHILE OTHERS LOOKED CALM AND CONFIDENT.

THE TWO FRIENDS WERE MOST INTRIGUED, WONDERING WHO WOULD BE THEIR PARTICULAR CHARGES...

LOOK AT THAT ONE, MAUREEN... SHE'S DROPPED ALL HER PACKAGES. REAL ZANY, I'D SAY.

SALLY WAS RIGHT. THE GIRL IN QUESTION WAS A COMPLETE SCATTERBRAIN.

DARN IT.. WHAT'S THE MATTER WITH THESE PARCELS?

SALLY TOOK THE GIRLS TO THE NURSES' COMMON ROOM WHERE SHE WAS ABLE TO CHAT AND GET TO KNOW THEM.

OH, I QUITE AGREE. NURSING IS DEFINITELY FOR THE CAREER GIRL.

GRACE IS A MUCH QUIETER VERSION OF IVY. I'D SAY SHE HAS THE MAKINGS OF A GOOD NURSE.

ON THE OTHER HAND, I CAN'T THINK WHY FIONA HAS DECIDED ON NURSING. SHE JUST ISN'T THE TYPE.

WHEN AT LAST SALLY WAS SATISFIED THAT THE GIRLS KNEW THEIR WAY AROUND THE HOSPITAL BUILDINGS, SHE DECIDED TO LEAVE THEM.

WELL AT LEAST YOU SHOULDN'T GET LOST WHEN ANYONE SENDS YOU ON AN ERRAND. DON'T FORGET WHAT I'VE TOLD YOU.

WE WON'T.

THAT NIGHT, SALLY AND MAUREEN SHARED THEIR IMPRESSIONS.

MY LOT ARE OKAY. WHAT ABOUT YOURS?

I HAVE A STRONG FEELING THAT I'M GOING TO HAVE TROUBLE WITH OUR BLONDE BOMBSHELL, FIONA.

THEY DANCED, AND SALLY WAS VERY MUCH AWARE OF CHESTER'S GOOD LOOKS AND CHARM.

I'M NOT VERY GOOD AT DANCING, I'M AFRAID.

YOU'RE DOING SPLENDIDLY.

SUDDENLY, HER ATTENTION WAS DIVERTED.

GOODNESS THAT'S FIONA, WITH ONE OF THE HOUSE-MEN. I DON'T SUPPOSE HE CAN AFFORD TO COME TO A PLACE LIKE THIS, BUT SHE WOULDN'T CARE.

THEY SAID GOODNIGHT, AND SALLY MADE NO OBJECTION WHEN CHESTER PULLED HER INTO HIS ARMS AND KISSED HER — VERY TENDERLY.

AS THE DAYS PASSED, SALLY BECAME CONVINCED THAT SHE WAS RIGHT. FIONA MADE A PLAY FOR ALL THE ELIGIBLE MEN OF THE HOSPITAL STAFF.

BUT ONE NIGHT THE ENTIRE HOSPITAL WAS AWAKENED TO A SPINE CHILLING HOWL....

A DOG IN THE GROUNDS! I MUST GO AND INVESTIGATE THIS FOR MYSELF.

AFTER THAT, GRACE APPEARED TO BE MUCH MORE SURE OF HERSELF...

AFTER THE ANAESTHETIC HAS BEEN ADMINISTERED I STAND TO ONE SIDE OF SISTER, ALERT AND READY TO DO WHATEVER SHE ASKS OF ME.

THAT'S THE IDEA, GRACE.

SALLY WAS OVERJOYED WITH HER PROGRESS...

OH, THERE'S NO DOUBT THAT SHE'S GOING TO MAKE A FIRST-CLASS NURSE.

DID YOU REALISE THAT SHE'S HAD SEVERAL DATES WITH CHESTER? YOU CERTAINLY STARTED SOMETHING THERE.

FORTUNATELY, GRACE DID NOT OVERHEAR, AND SALLY MANAGED TO KEEP HER OWN VOICE LOW WHEN...

IF YOU MUST KNOW, SHE HAS ALL THE QUALITIES THAT A MAN LOOKS FOR IN THE GIRL HE CHOOSES TO BE HIS WIFE... QUALITIES THAT YOU DON'T POSSESS, LET ME TELL YOU.

I THINK THAT'S GOING A BIT TOO FAR...

IT'S THE TRUTH, AND WHAT'S MORE GRACE IS CAPABLE OF LOVING A MAN FOR WHAT HE REALLY IS... I DON'T SUPPOSE YOU KNOW THE MEANING OF THE WORD.

REMEMBER THAT LOOKS AND A GOOD FIGURE AREN'T EVERYTHING... A GIRL HAS TO MAKE SACRIFICES, SHE HAS TO BE KIND AND UNDERSTANDING - AND YOU, FIONA, ARE QUITE INCAPABLE OF THESE THINGS.

FOR A MOMENT, FIONA WAS TOO STUNNED TO UTTER A WORD...

WHAT WAS IT MATRON HAD SAID?... 'ONLY ONE IN THREE OF THE GIRLS WOULD PROVE HERSELF.' FOR SALLY THE MOST UNLIKELY GIRL HAD SUCCEEDED.

EVERYONE WAS DELIGHTED WITH FIONA'S PROGRESS, AND SALLY COULD NOT HELP FEELING RATHER PROUD AND HAPPY — AS HAPPY AS A CERTAIN VET'S ASSISTANT... AND THE WIFE OF A YOUNG DOCTOR ABOARD A LINER BOUND FOR THE WEST INDIES.

PEARSON'S HOSPITAL NURSE PICTURE LIBRARY

A COLD MANNER MASKS A BROKEN HEART UNTIL NURSE SALLY BROWN FINDS A

CURE FOR DIANE

1/-

CURE FOR DIANE

PROBATIONARY NURSES SALLY BROWN AND MAUREEN EVANS HAD BEEN WORKING IN THE CHILDREN'S WARD FOR TWO WEEKS, AND IN SPITE OF EVERY EFFORT TO PLEASE, THEY HAD NOT BEEN ABLE TO BREAK THE RESERVE OF SISTER DIANE GRIERSON WHO WAS IN CHARGE.

WE'LL INCREASE LITTLE LIONEL BARRY'S INJECTIONS TO TWO A DAY. OTHERWISE CARRY ON WITH TREATMENTS AS BEFORE.

YES SISTER.

I'M NOT MAKING MUCH SENSE, I KNOW. BUT I'LL PROVE TO YOU WHAT I MEAN ONE OF THESE DAYS. YOU SEE IF I DON'T.

IT WAS EASIER TO CHAT WHEN THE PATIENTS WERE TOO YOUNG TO LISTEN, ALL THE SAME SALLY AND MAUREEN WORKED HARD...

DON'T YOU FEEL A NICE CLEAN BOY, AFTER YOUR BATH, BOBBY? AND NOW IT'S BACK TO BED.

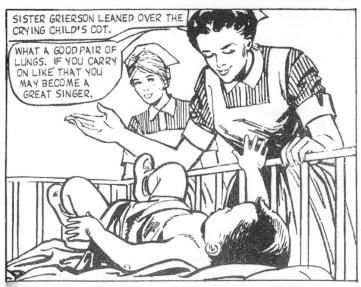

SHE'S CERTAINLY GOT A WAY WITH KIDS.

HANG AROUND, MAUREEN, AND WATCH SISTER THAW COMPLETELY. SHE'S NOT SUCH AN ICEBERG AFTER ALL, EH?

WHAT SORT OF STORY IS IT?

ONE THAT'S SPECIAL FOR GOOD BOYS LIKE YOU.

SISTER REMAINED QUITE UNAWARE OF HER AUDIENCE...

ONCE UPON A TIME THERE WAS A LITTLE BOY WHO WAS TOO POOR TO OWN A PAIR OF SHOES...

DIDN'T HE CRY?

OF COURSE NOT. ONLY BABIES CRY.

WILLIAM WAS SOON FAST ASLEEP.

WELL, SHE DIDN'T TAKE LONG TO CHARM THAT LITTLE IMP.

AND HOW SHE CHANGED. SHE BEGAN TO LOOK ALMOST HUMAN.

THAT SAME AFTERNOON, SISTER WAS FORGOTTEN IN THE EXCITEMENT OF A FEW HOURS OFF DUTY. MAUREEN WAS DEAD KEEN ON A TWIST SESSION ADVERTISED IN TOWN WHILE SALLY WANTED TO BUY CILLA BLACK'S LATEST POP HIT.

I'M NEARLY READY.

AND ABOUT TIME TOO. WHY DOES IT TAKE YOU SO LONG?

IT WAS STANDING ROOM ONLY ON THE BUS INTO TOWN, BUT TRUST MAUREEN TO FIND A REAL GEAR FELLOW.

I THINK THERE OUGHT TO BE MORE STANDING ROOM ON THESE BUSES, DON'T YOU?

LARGE BUSES WOULD MAKE MANOEUVRING A PROBLEM.

BY THE END OF THE JOURNEY, THE WEATHER LEFT NO-ONE IN DOUBT — IT WAS RAINING TORRENTS!

QUICK, MAUREEN, WE'LL HAVE TO TAKE COVER UNTIL THIS EASES.

JUST A MINUTE, YOU CAN SHARE MY UMBRELLA, IT'S QUITE LARGE.

NO JOKE. I WORK IN THE NEXT BLOCK OF OFFICES. I'M A SECRETARY AND MY BOSS MR. VANE WILL BE EXPECTING ME IN TWO MINUTES.

WELL, WHAT DO YOU KNOW?

THE YOUNG MAN HURRIED AWAY, TAKING HIS UMBRELLA WITH HIM.

BYE GIRLS, NICE MEETING YOU. BASIL WATT IS THE NAME. HOPE WE CAN SEE EACH OTHER AGAIN, SOMETIME.

SALLY AND MAUREEN WOULD HAVE BEEN SURPRISED IF THEY COULD HAVE GUESSED HER THOUGHTS.

I WONDER IF MEN AND WOMEN IN THOSE EARLY AGES WERE CAPABLE OF FEELING THE PAIN OF HOPELESS LOVE.

THE RAIN WAS EASING OFF WHEN DIANE DECIDED TO LEAVE THE MUSEUM...

TAXI!

ALWAYS CONCERNED FOR HER LITTLE PATIENTS, SHE NOW WANTED TO RETURN TO THEM AS QUICKLY AS POSSIBLE.

THE GENERAL HOSPITAL, PLEASE.

SALLY AND MAUREEN WATCHED HER GO...

HOW OLD DO YOU THINK SHE IS, SAL?

DIFFICULT TO SAY, BUT WHEN SHE SMILED AT LITTLE WILLIAM SHE LOOKED UNDER THIRTY.

MMMM, BUT GENERALLY SHE LOOKS MUCH OLDER — NOT THE TYPE TO MAKE A MAN LOOK TWICE. I DON'T SUPPOSE SHE WANTS THEM TO BOTHER ANYWAY.

THE AFTERNOON WASTED, SALLY AND MAUREEN RETURNED TO THE NURSES HOME, WHERE THEY DECIDED TO HAVE AN EARLY NIGHT... AND STILL IT RAINED.

WHAT A MISERABLE DAY... IT HASN'T STOPPED, ALTHOUGH I DON'T SUPPOSE DIANE GRIERSON NOTICED.

THE FOLLOWING MORNING, IT WAS BACK ON DUTY — AND THE DAY WAS BRIGHT AND SUNNY!

WE'VE GOT A CASE OF SCARLET FEVER COMING INTO THE ISOLATION WARD, SO EVERYTHING MUST BE MADE READY IN DOUBLE QUICK TIME. LET'S SEE, THE CHILD'S NAME IS...

SISTER PALED, AND WHEN SHE SPOKE AGAIN HER VOICE WAS A WHISPER...

CAROLINE VANE... DAUGHTER OF ANTHONY AND SARAH.

ANYTHING WRONG, SISTER?

CAROLINE VANE WAS SOON OCCUPYING THE BED. SHE WAS AN ATTRACTIVE CHILD, IN SPITE OF THE FEVER WHICH HAD MADE HER SO ILL.

HER FATHER WAS OBVIOUSLY VERY WORRIED.

I KNOW SHE IS IN GOOD HANDS, BUT I HATE THE IDEA OF LEAVING HER LIKE THIS.

I'M AFRAID I MUST ASK YOU TO GO. SHE NEEDS REST AND QUIET.

I UNDERSTAND.

SISTER GRIERSON STOOD IN THE DOORWAY, UNDECIDED ABOUT COMING INTO THE ROOM.

BUT SHE COULD NOT ESCAPE...

DIANE! I HAD NO IDEA THAT YOU WERE WORKING HERE.

IT'S BEEN A LONG TIME SINCE WE WERE IN TOUCH, BUT YOU WERE OFF TO EDINBURGH THEN.

YES, I STAYED THERE THREE YEARS BEFORE COMING SOUTH TO THIS HOSPITAL. REST ASSURED THAT WE WILL DO OUR BEST FOR YOUR LITTLE DAUGHTER.

SALLY SLIPPED OUT...

I RECKON THEY HAVEN'T SEEN EACH OTHER FOR SOMETHING LIKE EIGHT YEARS.

THEY MUST HAVE BEEN MORE THAN GOOD FRIENDS. OTHERWISE SISTER WOULDN'T HAVE BEEN SO UPSET WHEN SHE READ THE NAME.

IN THE COMMON ROOM, MAUREEN WAS ANSWERING THE TELEPHONE.

YES, SIR. I CAN GET IN TOUCH WITH THE CHILDREN'S WARD. WHO DID YOU WANT?

IT WAS SOME MOMENTS BEFORE THEIR TELEPHONE CONVERSATION CAME TO AN END, AND THE MESSAGE FOR MR. VANE HAD BY THEN BEEN FORGOTTEN.

WEREN'T YOU SUPPOSED TO BE TELLING MR. VANE SOMETHING?

YES, BUT...

DON'T LOOK SO GUILTY. MR. VANE IS LEAVING NOW, ANYWAY.

IS THAT SO.

SALLY FOUND SISTER GRIERSON, ALONE — AND CRYING...

EXCUSE ME SISTER, BUT I'D LIKE TO HELP YOU. I REALISE THAT BOTH YOU AND LITTLE CAROLINE HAVE JUST HEARD SOME RATHER UPSETTING NEWS.

I WAS A FOOL SALLY. I TRIED TO DREAM UP A CASTLE IN THE AIR...! BUT IT SHATTERED EVEN MORE QUICKLY THAN THE LAST TIME.

DIANE GRIERSON TURNED TO SALLY FOR COMFORT...

YOU LOVE ANTHONY VANE A GREAT DEAL, DON'T YOU?

I WAS VERY YOUNG WHEN I FIRST FELT ATTRACTED TOWARDS TONY VANE. THEN ONE DAY, MY BEST FRIEND SARAH TOLD ME SHE WAS HEAD OVER HEELS IN LOVE WITH HIM. THAT WAS WHEN I WALKED OUT OF THEIR LIVES.

I WILLINGLY MADE THE SACRIFICE FOR MY FRIEND, BUT FATE CAN BE SO UNKIND, DON'T YOU THINK? THANKS FOR YOUR UNDERSTANDING, SALLY.

I BELIEVE TONY VANE WAS DEEPLY IN LOVE WITH DIANE GRIERSON. HIS TROUBLE IS THAT HE'S TRYING TO FORGET.

BUT WE MUSTN'T LET HIM, EH?

THAT'S THE IDEA, BUT WE'LL HAVE TO MOVE VERY CAREFULLY.

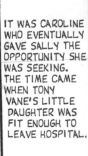

IT WAS CAROLINE WHO EVENTUALLY GAVE SALLY THE OPPORTUNITY SHE WAS SEEKING. THE TIME CAME WHEN TONY VANE'S LITTLE DAUGHTER WAS FIT ENOUGH TO LEAVE HOSPITAL.

HAPPY TO BE COMING HOME?

YES, IF YOU PROMISE ME SOMETHING.

WHAT'S THAT?

MAUREEN FOLLOWED SALLY TO THE ROOM THEY SHARED.

WE'VE DONE IT SAL. SHE DIDN'T EVEN PROTEST ABOUT THAT DRESS. NOW WE SHALL SEE.

THE PARTY HAD ALREADY STARTED WHEN DIANE ARRIVED. CYNTHIA STUART WAS BORED AND MADE NO EFFORT TO HIDE THE FACT.

THESE KIDS HAVE GIVEN ME A DREADFUL HEADACHE.

IT'S THEIR PARTY, MY DEAR. YOU MUST EXPECT THEM TO LET OFF STEAM.

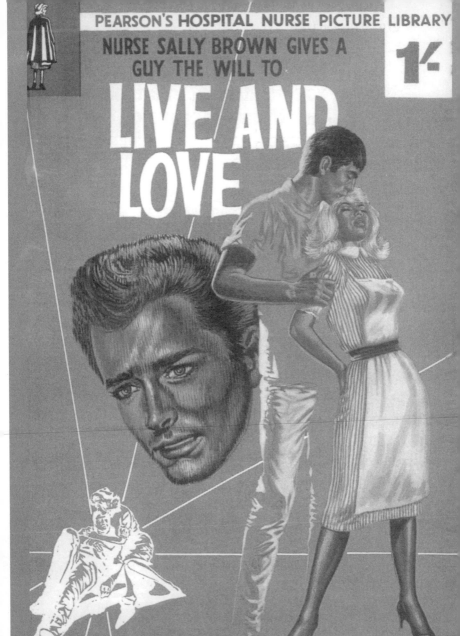

PEARSON'S **HOSPITAL** NURSE PICTURE LIBRARY

1'-

NURSE SALLY BROWN GIVES A
GUY THE WILL TO

LIVE AND
LOVE

THE SENIOR HOSPITAL STAFF DID NOT HAVE MUCH TO DO WITH ITS YOUNGER AND MORE JUNIOR MEMBERS, SO WHEN DR. JAMES SPOKE DIRECTLY TO SALLY, SHE WAS TAKEN BY SURPRISE.

WHAT'S YOUR NAME, NURSE?

OH, DR. JAMES... SALLY...

WHAT'S THE MATTER DOCTOR?

THE DOCTOR IGNORED CHRIS'S QUESTION.

NURSE, REPORT TO ME IN MY OFFICE IN ABOUT HALF-AN-HOUR'S TIME.

YES, OF COURSE, DOCTOR.

WHAT WAS ALL THAT ABOUT? HAS MY FAVOURITE NURSE BEEN DOING SOMETHING SHE SHOULDN'T?

SEARCH ME... UNLESS HE HEARD US TALKING AND LAUGHING TOGETHER AND DISAPPROVED.

TO PUT IT BLUNTLY, WE WANT YOU TO STAY WITH HIM ALL THE WHILE... TO PANDER TO HIS EVERY WISH... AND IN YOUR OWN FEMININE WAY GIVE HIM SOMETHING TO LIVE FOR... SO THAT HE WILL BE AGREEABLE TO HAVING THE NEXT OPERATION, AND WE HOPE FULLY RECOVER. NOW IT'S UP TO YOU. WHAT DO YOU SAY?

SALLY READILY AGREED WITH THE DOCTORS SCHEME, AND LATER TOLD AN ANXIOUS MAUREEN ALL THAT HAD HAPPENED.

HECK, SOME GIRLS HAVE ALL THE LUCK! JUST THINK YOU'LL BE RELIEVED OF ALL YOUR OTHER DUTIES SO THAT YOU CAN DEVOTE YOURSELF ENTIRELY TO CHRIS. WHAT A MARVELLOUS JOB.

HOLD ON, MAUREEN, THERE ARE CERTAIN DRAWBACKS. WHAT IF HE GETS TOO INTERESTED IN ME? I MAY NOT LIKE THE IDEA, BUT I SHALL STILL HAVE TO PRETEND THAT I DO.

MIDNIGHT SALLY WAS NO NEARER A SOLUTION TO HER PROBLEM. MAUREEN WAS DESPERATE FOR SLEEP.

LOOK, SAL, DO ME A FAVOUR. MARRY YOUR RICH AND HANDSOME CHRIS AND LET ME GET SOME SLEEP.

OKAY, MAUREEN, YOU'VE MADE YOUR POINT, BUT IF YOU HAD MY WORRIES I BET YOU WOULD BE AS BOTHERED AS I AM.

NEXT MORNING SALLY WAS ON DUTY AS USUAL... ALTHOUGH SHE COULD NOT HELP FEELING THAT SOMETHING DECISIVE WAS GOING TO HAPPEN.

AND HER FEMININE INTUITION PROVED HER RIGHT...

COME, CLOSER SALLY... BECAUSE I WANT TO TELL YOU THAT YOU'RE THE MOST IMPORTANT THING THAT'S HAPPENED IN MY LIFE.

OH, CHRIS.

HE PULLED HER INTO HIS ARMS. AND THE SWEET PASSIONATE KISS THAT FOLLOWED INCREASED SALLY'S DOUBTS.

MY DARLING SWEETHEART.

OH...

THEATRE

TO SALLY, THE HOURS THAT FOLLOWED WERE LIKE A NIGHTMARE...HER HEART ACHED FOR THE MAN WHO WAS NOW INVOLVED IN A TREMENDOUS BATTLE BETWEEN LIFE AND DEATH.

FINALLY...

YOU'LL BE GLAD TO HEAR THAT THE OPERATION WAS SUCCESSFUL NURSE. THANKS TO YOU,OUR PATIENT PUT UP A TERRIFIC FIGHT WHICH SAVED HIM.

WHAT A RELIEF. OH, DOCTOR, I'M SO GLAD.

I MUST, OF COURSE, POINT OUT THAT HE'S GOT TO TAKE THINGS VERY EASY FOR THE NEXT SIX MONTHS OR SO... ANY WORRIES OR SHOCKS WOULD UNDOUBTEDLY SET HIM BACK. DO YOU UNDERSTAND?

PERFECTLY. I'LL MAKE CERTAIN HE'S NOT UPSET, DOCTOR.

PRESENTLY CHRIS JOINED HER...

WELL, WHAT DO YOU THINK OF IT, DARLING? WOULD YOU LIKE TO SEE THE INSIDE?

YES, CHRIS, I WOULD, BUT I MUSTN'T STAY TOO LONG. I'VE GOT A SPELL OF DUTY THIS EVENING.

THE HOUSE WAS VERY TASTEFULLY FURNISHED AND SALLY WAS CONTINUALLY THRILLED AS SHE WALKED FROM ROOM TO ROOM. THAT WAY TIME WHIZZED BY, AND ALL TOO SOON CHRIS WAS DRIVING HER BACK.

AS SOON AS THE DOCTORS AGREE, YOU'LL HAVE TO START GOING TO PARTIES AND MIXING WITH PEOPLE.

THAT'S A WONDERFUL IDEA, SALLY, ESPECIALLY WITH YOU TO PARTNER ME. YES, I'M CERTAINLY LOOKING FORWARD TO PAINTING THE TOWN...

THEY DANCED... THEY DINED... THEY WENT TO THEATRES AND CINEMAS, BUT ALTHOUGH THEY MET LOTS OF PEOPLE, CHRIS STILL ONLY HAD EYES FOR SALLY.

SALLY BACKED AWAY LEAVING THEM TO TALK TOGETHER. WAS THIS THE OPPORTUNITY SHE HAD BEEN WAITING FOR SO LONG?

SUSAN WAS OBVIOUSLY ONE OF HIS OLD FLAMES. I WONDER IF THEY STILL FEEL ANYTHING FOR EACH OTHER, AND WHETHER HE'LL WANT TO SEE MORE OF HER? I'LL TRY AND THROW THEM TOGETHER.

THIS WAS WHY THE NEXT TIME CHRIS TELEPHONED SALLY AT THE HOSPITAL...

SORRY, CHRIS, I JUST CAN'T MAKE IT THIS EVENING, I'VE GOT TOO MUCH TO DO. COULDN'T YOU TAKE SUSAN OUT INSTEAD?

HECK, SHE MUST BE MAD.

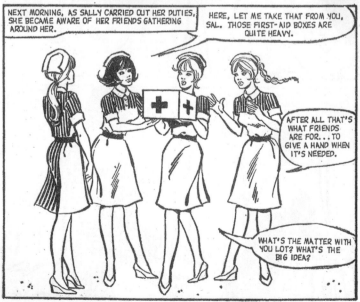

BUT I WANT TO FEEL BADLY ABOUT IT. PERHAPS HE WAS IN LOVE AS I AM, WITH EVERY HOPE FOR A BRIGHT AND WONDERFUL FUTURE, AND THEN HE'S STRUCK DOWN BY THIS FILTHY TROPICAL DISEASE.

I'M GLAD YOU INSISTED THAT WE WENT TO HEAR THAT LECTURE... IT'S MADE ME REALISE WHAT A MISERABLY SMALL AND PETTY LIFE I LEAD.

DON'T SAY THINGS LIKE THAT, DARLING.

IN LESS THAN AN HOUR, SHE WALKED BACK THROUGH THE HOSPITAL GATES... A LITTLE SAD PERHAPS BECAUSE GOOD-BYES ALWAYS MADE HER CRY. BUT IN SPITE OF THIS, QUIETLY CONFIDENT THAT SHE HAD DONE THE RIGHT THING IN LETTING HER BOYFRIEND PURSUE A VOCATION WHICH COULD BECOME AS IMPORTANT AS HER OWN. AND, ANYWAY, THERE WAS EVERY CHANCE THAT THEY WOULD MEET AGAIN, WASN'T THERE?

1/-

BLUES FOR A BEAT BOY

A CASUALTY
ON THE
ROAD TO FAME
MEETS
A NURSE
WITH LOVE
IN HER
HEART

SALLY'S FRIEND, MAUREEN WHO HAD BEEN WATCHING FROM ONE OF THE HOSPITAL WINDOWS CAME OUT TO MEET HER...

HAVEN'T YOU HEARD? GOODNESS I SHOULD'VE THOUGHT YOU WOULD HAVE REALISED. WE'VE GOT A BEAT GROUP IN THE HOSPITAL... THEY WERE ALL INVOLVED IN AN ACCIDENT.

BUT WHY DO I HAVE TO BE CHASED BY THEIR FANS? WHAT'S IT GOT TO DO WITH ME?

QUITE A LOT, MY DEAR SALLY. YOU HAVE BEEN CHOSEN FOR DUTY IN THE GROUPS WARD... ALTHOUGH I DON'T SUPPOSE FOR ONE MOMENT THAT THE FANS REALISED THAT.

GRACIOUS! AND IS OUR BEAT GROUP ALL THAT FAMOUS? HAVE I HEARD OF THEM?

SALLY ENTEPED THE WARD, SECRETLY THRILLED AT THE IDEA OF MEETING THE GEARMEN FACE TO FACE... AFTER ALL THEY WERE THE MOST POPULAR GROUP IN THE COUNTRY.

THEY LOOK JUST LIKE THEIR PICTURES, IF A BIT SHAKEN UP AT THE MOMENT.

THE GEARMEN WERE DELIGHTED WHEN THEY LEARNED THAT SALLY WOULD BE LOOKING AFTER THEM...

HEY, WHY DON'T YOU JOIN US PERMANENTLY AS MEDICAL ADVISER? WE'D LIKE A LITTLE CHICK LIKE YOU TO TAKE OUR TEMPERATURES FROM TIME TO TIME, AND HOLD OUR HANDS, OF COURSE.

THIS SUDDEN TURN OF EVENTS WAS THE ONLY TOPIC OF CONVERSATION AMONGST THE YOUNG NURSES...

BUT WHAT'S GOING TO BECOME OF THE GROUP? RIFF IS TERRIFIC... THE GEARMEN WILL BE NOTHING WITHOUT HIM.

I DON'T KNOW WHAT'S GOING TO HAPPEN, BUT ONE THING'S FOR SURE, RIFF WANTS TO WASH HIS HANDS OF THE GROUP.

MEANWHILE, SAM WAS LOOKING LIKE A RUINED MAN...

CHEER UP SAM, THERE MUST BE A WAY OUT... HAVE YOU NOTICED HOW HE'S BEEN LOOKING AT OUR PRETTY NURSE?

IT WON'T HELP FELLERS. RIFF WON'T CHANGE HIS MIND NOW.

AND WHEN THE FANS HAD BEEN FORCIBLY REMOVED FROM THE HOSPITAL, AND ALL WAS QUIET AGAIN, SALLY HAD A WORD WITH MAUREEN.

MATRON'S FURIOUS, BUT IT WASN'T MY FAULT... I COULDN'T STOP THEM GETTING IN.

AND IT'S NOT THE GEARMEN'S FAULT. THEY CAN'T HELP BEING SO POPULAR.

THEY WON'T BE POPULAR FOR VERY MUCH LONGER, I'M THINKING, IF RIFF CARRIES OUT HIS THREAT TO LEAVE THE GROUP.

DO YOU THINK HE REALLY MEANS IT, SAL? OR IS HE JUST SAYING THAT TO GET SOME PERSONAL PUBLICITY.

IT WAS ALMOST MIDNIGHT WHEN A MINI-VAN SPED THROUGH THE HOSPITAL GATES WITH THE GEARMEN AND THEIR INSTRUMENTS ABOARD...

THEY ARRIVED AT THE HOTEL WHERE SAM WAS WAITING TO GREET THEM.

IT'S ALL CLEAR BOYS... NO ONE ABOUT... SO MAKE IT SLIPPY.